I0648546

Mary Hannay Black Foott

Morna Lee

And other Poems. Second Edition

Mary Hannay Black Foott

Morna Lee
And other Poems. Second Edition

ISBN/EAN: 9783337401405

Printed in Europe, USA, Canada, Australia, Japan

Cover: Foto ©Andreas Hilbeck / pixelio.de

More available books at **www.hansebooks.com**

MORNA LEE

AND

OTHER POEMS.

BY

MARY HANNAY FOOTT.

SECOND EDITION.

London:

GORDON & GOTCH, PUBLISHERS, ST. BRIDE STREET.

BRISBANE: GORDON & GOTCH, QUEEN STREET

ALSO AT SYDNEY AND MELBOURNE.

1890.

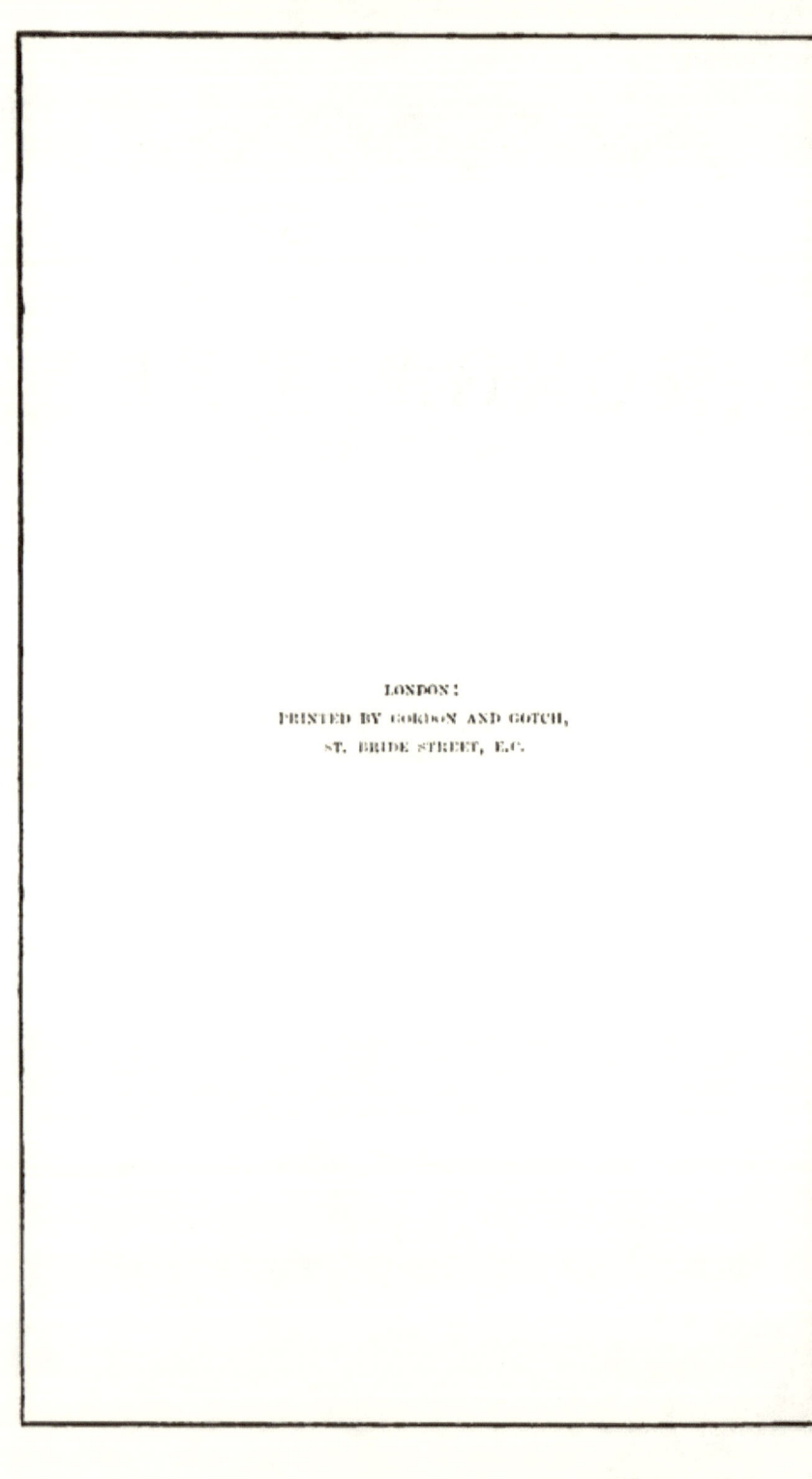

LONDON:
PRINTED BY GORDON AND GOTCH,
ST. BRIDE STREET, E.C.

PREFACE TO SECOND EDITION.

—————

THE very kind reception accorded both by the Press and the public to the former volume of the Author's poems has induced her to offer a second edition, including several of her later compositions.

Brisbane, 1889.

CONTENTS.

I.

(AUSTRALIAN POEMS.)

CONTENTS.

V.
(TRANSLATIONS.)

VI.

VII.

VIII.
(POEMS FOR CHILDREN).

⊹ POEMS. ⊹

Morna Lee.

JOHN WARRISTON rode through the mulga scrub, and the
    gravel shone black and bare,
For the long white mulga grass was gone, and no dew nor
    rain came there.
He rode by the shady gidya-camps, where the cattle had
    crawled to die,
And by creeks that failed ere the summer came, and
    lagoons that had long been dry—
Where the bones of the beasts that had perished lay a-
    bleach in the brick burnt mire,
And the ground was aglow 'neath old Emperor's hoofs, and
    the wind was the breath of fire.

John Warriston rode with a heavy heart and a slackening
    wrist and knee,
For the loss that faced him on every side and the thought
    of Morna Lee.

" Morna Lee, had your lot been cast with mine, in these
    days of woe,
I had feared not the fiercest suns that shine nor the bitterest
    winds that blow.

What to us were my mother's taunt that of gipsy race you
    came—
My father's ban, or my brother's scorn, or my sister's
    gentle blame?
I braved them all for your bright brown eyes and the love
    betwixt us twain;
And I dreamed that you would defy them too—but, alas,
    my dream was vain.
So the tress you gave when our troth was new and the ring
    you would not wear
Are all that shall ever be mine and yours—till I meet you
    otherwhere.

"I thought to forget you, and I wed, and my bride was
    fond and fair—
The boy she bore has her soft blue eyes, and her smile, and
    her sunny hair;
But her spirit sank in this wilderness, and I sent her over sea
To the kin she longed for as I long for my one love—
    Morna Lee."

Old Emperor halted. His master ceased from his musing
    sad and vain;
And he gazed around on the drought-cursed ground with a
    prayer in his heart for rain.
"Not for my sake, O God," he said, "but for theirs do I
    seek Thy grace—
For the mother and babe whose heritage Thou makest a
    barren place."

A touch—so light it was scarce a touch—of the rider's
    rowelled heel,
But erst 'twas enough for the old horse—now he stood to
    the stinging steel;

Till Warriston woke from the maze of care and saw what
    his steed had seen—
A wild mare left by her troop to die, where the waters once
    had been.

Too weak to follow her kin in quest of the streams that
    flowed afar,
Famine and thirst would have done their worst ere the
    wane of the even star.
Staring now was her sable coat and wistful her fearless
    eye;
John Warriston watched her as she lay, till he could not
    pass her by.
Swift he unbuckled the water-bag that hung at his saddle-
    bow—
" Emperor and I can want for once; this draught is the
    wild mare's now."

He opened her mouth and he made her drink—for she
    lacked the strength to flee—
And her look in his face, as he left her side, was the look
    of Morna Lee.

With the empty bag at his saddle-bow, he mounted and
    rode away
At the utmost speed of the good gray steed that had
    carried him many a day:
But he halted again at the hill-side camp, and let the old
    horse go;
And he lit his fire and smoked his pipe, and gazed on the
    after-glow

Till the rhythmic beat of the trammelled feet grew faint,
 and afar was heard
The tuneless bell, as if sweet notes fell from the throat of
 the chime-voiced bird.

     *   *   *   *   *   *

He dreamt as he slept that a spirit swept from the swelter-
 ing Indian seas,
And her misty pinions veiled the moon and her trailing
 robes the trees.
And he woke to the scent of the sandalwood, and knew
 that, once again,
There had flown from the East, for man and beast, the
 Angel of the Rain.

A wind—sea-born of the wild monsoon—a flash like the
 heavens aflame—
A thunder-crash like the crash of Doom, and the wished-
 for waters came.

John Warriston waited not for the dawn on the tracks of
 the good old gray,
For a dam that yet had never been wet must stand or fall
 that day :
And he passed, with a heart that was praising Heaven,
 through the floods he could not see,
And a pitiful thought for the perishing beast with the eyes
 of Morna Lee.

     *   *   *   *   *   *

The fresh filled creeks ran redly yet, and yellow and white
 anew
Tall lilies rose from the green morass, and the nesting wild-
 fowl flew ;

When with broken hobbles and tongueless bell, and the
    long familiar stride,
Emperor came to the station-rails with the wild mare at his
    side.

Wife to cherish, or child to cheer, in that lonely house was
    none.
Toil and rest and the night-long guest were the sum from
    sun to sun.
But the tender touch of his lean brown hand on the
    flowers it cherished fell,
Fonder yet on each household pet and the horse that had
    served him well.
Fonder than all, when, slim and tall, the wild thing
    trembling came,
On the head that pressed his forsaken breast, whilst he
    called her by her name.

    *   *   *   *   *   *

"Seven years of plenty! There were need of another seven
    beside,
That the brand of the drought may fade from out the land
    that Heavenward cried
So long in vain for the blessed rain. And the second seven
    may be"
John Warriston mused by his lonely hearth — "but they
    will not profit me.
Another shall claim the herds I kept 'neath the frost and
    the tropic beam.
His flocks shall drink at the dams I saved waist-deep in the
    midnight stream.
Where I watched with a heartsick prayer to Heaven, he may
    sleep, with no prayer denied;
But one name that I loved he shall never learn — one horse
    that I rode ne'er ride.

One, for the mound is green above the bones of the gallant
    gray,
And the wild mare goes with me where I go, or stays where
    he must stay."

The muster began ere the morning broke; and neighbour
    and friend were there;
But Warriston rode for the boy he loved, and the far-off
    wife and fair:
And the black mare answered the urging heel as never did
    mare before;
But she fell in her leap where the bank was steep—and he
    knew he should ride no more.

     *   *   *   *   *   *

John Warriston lay in the darkened room; he was dying and
    could not die;
Day after day he had heard the shouts as the cattle were
    driven by;
Day after day, as the slow sum grew, he dreaded the coming
    day—
Horses were failing and riders spent, and half of the herd
    away.

Over the ranges they brought them back, and out from the
    brigalow,
And from under the giant gums that mark where the
    frequent waters flow.
They quitted their fires ere the stars were quenched—they
    camped on the creek at noon;
And the station rails like silver shone at the rising of the
    moon.

What was it frighted the timorous herd?—The bay of the
    tethered hound?—
The chant of the swarthy mother above the babe that her
    arms enwound?

For the mighty mass was riven and shed, like a raft that
    parts at sea;
And where was the horse that should head them now?
    and the rider, where was he?

John Warriston heard the wild stampede, and he shattered
    the shutter bar,
And gazed on the flying herd without and the moveless
    moon and star.
" Pray for the boy that is beggared now—if room in
    Heaven there be
For the love that recks not of thine and mine, O Morna—
    Morna Lee!"

A shadow athwart the cloudless moon—a check in the
    headlong speed
Of the broken ranks; they are steadied now—they are
    stayed by a riderless steed—
Till the horsemen rally; and one and all are pent in the
    yards ere day;
But the dew shall dry from their mossy hides and the
    brands unreddened stay.

For in hush of the homestead whispering the bearded bush-
    men tell
Of the gallop that shamed them all—and killed the steed
    that he loved so well.
And the dirge of a savage race rings high where the white
    man's grave shall be;
And the harpies haste where the brave heart broke of the
    wild mare—Morna Lee.

Brisbane, 4th November, 1886.

𝕎here the 𝕡elican 𝔹uilds.

[The unexplored parts of Australia are sometimes spoken of by the bushmen of Western Queensland as the home of the pelican, a bird whose nesting place, so far as the writer knows, is seldom, if ever found.]

THE horses were ready, the rails were down,
  But the riders lingered still—
    One had a parting word to say,
  And one had his pipe to fill.
Then they mounted, one with a granted prayer,
  And one with a grief unguessed.
    "We are going," they said, as they rode away—
  "Where the pelican builds her nest!"

They had told us of pastures wide and green,
  To be sought past the sunset's glow;
    Of rifts in the ranges by opal lit:
  And gold 'neath the river's flow.
And thirst and hunger were banished words
  When they spoke of that unknown West;
    No drought they dreaded, no flood they feared,
  Where the pelican builds her nest!

The creek at the ford was but fetlock deep
  When we watched them crossing there:
    The rains have replenished it thrice since then,
  And thrice has the rock lain bare.
But the waters of Hope have flowed and fled,
  And never from blue hill's breast
    Come back—by the sun and the sands devoured—
  Where the pelican builds her nest!

" New Country."

Condie had come with us all the way—
  Eight hundred miles but the fortnight's rest
Made him fresh as a youngster, the sturdy bay!
  And Lurline was looking her very best.

Weary and footsore, the cattle strayed
  'Mid the silvery saltbush well content ;
Where the creeks lay cool 'neath the gidya's shade
  The stock-horses clustered, travel-spent.

In the bright spring morning we left them all
  Camp, and cattle, and white, and black—
And rode for the Range's westward fall,
  Where the dingo's trail was the only track.

Slow through the clay-pans, wet to the knee,
  With the cane-grass rustling overhead ;
Swift o'er the plains with never a tree ;
  Up the cliffs by a torrent's bed.

Bridle on arm for a mile or more
  We toiled, ere we reached Biadanna's verge
And saw—as one sees a far-off shore—
  The blue hills bounding the forest surge.

An ocean of trees, by the west wind stirred,
  Rolled, ever rolled, to the great cliff's base ;
And its sound like the noise of waves was heard
  'Mid the rocks and the caves of that lonely place.

   *   *   *   *   *   *

We recked not of wealth in stream or soil
  As we heard on the heights the breezes sing ;
We felt no longer our travel-toil ;
  We feared no more what the years might bring.

14th March, 1889.

Up North.*

Into Thy hands let me fall, O Lord—
    Not into the hands of men—
And she thinned the ranks of the savage horde
    Till they shrank to the mangrove fen.

In a rudderless boat, with a scanty store
    Of food for the fated three—
With her babe and her stricken servitor
    She fled to the open sea.

Oh, days of dolor and nights of drouth,
    While she watched for a sail in vain,
Or the tawny tinge of a river mouth,
    Or the rush of the tropic rain.

The valiant woman! Her feeble oar
    Sufficed, and her fervent prayer
Was heard, though she reached but a barren shore,
    And died with her darling there.

For the demons of murder and foul disgrace
    On her hearthstone dared not light;
But the Angel of Womanhood held the place,
    And its site is a holy site.

* The incident referred to in the above poem took place a few years ago in one of the small islands off the northern coast of Queensland. Mrs. Watson, wife of a bêche de mer fisher, was left, in her husband's absence, with her infant child and two Chinese servants on the island. The homestead was attacked by wild blacks from the mainland, one of the servants killed, and the other wounded. Mrs. Watson defended her home so effectually with her revolver that the assailants withdrew. Fearing their return she placed some little provision in an iron tank, which had been cut down so that it served as a boat, and embarking in this frail vessel, with her child and the wounded man, she strove to make her way to some place of refuge. The tank was found some time afterwards on the shore of an uninhabited and waterless island, where the remains of the ill-fated voyagers were also discovered. Mrs. Watson kept a diary almost up to the last.

In the Land of Dreams.

A BRIDLE-PATH in the tangled mallee,
  With blossoms unnamed and unknown bespread—
And two who ride through its leafy alley—
  But never the sound of a horse's tread.

And one by one whilst the foremost rider
  Puts back the boughs which have grown apace,
And side by side where the track is wider
  Together they come to the olden place.

To the leaf-dyed pool whence the mallards fluttered,
  Or ever the horses had paused to drink ;
Where the word was said and the vow was uttered
  That brighten for ever its weedy brink.

And Memory closes her sad recital—
  In Fate's cold eyes there are kindly gleams—
While for one brief moment of blest requital
  The parted have met— in the Land of Dreams.

13th June, 1882.

Happy Days.

A FRINGE of rushes—one green line
  Upon a faded plain ;
A silver streak of water-shine—
  Above, tree-watchers twain.
It was our resting-place awhile,
  And still, with backward gaze,
We say : "Tis many a weary mile—
  But there were happy days."

And shall no ripple break the sand
   Upon our farther way?
Or reedy ranks all knee-deep stand?
   Or leafy tree-tops sway?
The gold of dawn is surely met
   In sunset's lavish blaze;
And— in horizons hidden yet—
   There shall be happy days.

In Time of Drought.

"The river of God is full of water."— Psalm.

THE rushes are black by the river bed,
   And the sheep and the cattle stand,
Wistful-eyed, where the waters were,
   In a waste of gravel and sand:
Or pass o'er their dying and dead to slake
   Their thirst at the slimy pool.
Shall they pine and perish in pangs of drought
   While Thy river, O God, is full?

The fields are furrowed, the seed is sown,
   But no dews from the heavens are shed;
And where shall the grain for the harvest be?
   And how shall the poor be fed?
In waterless gullies they winnow the earth,
   New-turned by the miner's tool:
And the wayfarer faints 'neath his lightened load* —
   Yet the river of God is full.

* During a drought, travellers sometimes have to throw away even their
blankets and any superfluous clothing.

For us, O Father, from tropic seas,
   Let the clouds be filled that shed
Rough rains upon Andes' eastward slope,
   Soft snows on Himáleh's head.
Freight for us as for others thy dark-winged
     fleet,
   That soon by the waters cool
We may say with gladness: "Our need was
     great,
   But the river of God was full!"

"He Sendeth His Rain."

FRESH leaflets tinge the gray gum's crest;
   Young grass makes green the russet plain;
Again the wild duck seeks her nest;
   The bell bird's note is heard again.

And soft blue mist-wrack floats afar
   At eve, from waters gathering yet;
And bright beneath the morning star
   The dewy woodlands glister wet.

Glad Autumn of a joyless year,
   Thee wood and stream and wildling bless;
And they no less thy dews hold dear
   Whom Heaven hath heard in their distress.

The Aurora Australis.

A RADIANCE in the midnight sky
   No white moon gave, nor yellow star ;
We thought its red glow mounted high
   Where fire and forest fought afar,

Half questioning if the township blazed,
   Perchance, beyond the boundary hill :
Then, finding what it was, we gazed
   And wondered till we shivered chill.

And Fancy showed the sister-glow
   Of our Aurora, sending lines
Of lustre forth to tint the snow
   That lodges in Norwegian pines.

And South and North alternate swept
   In vision past us, to and fro ;
While stealthy winds of midnight crept
   About us, whispering fast and low.

The North, whose star burns steadily,
   High set in heaven long ago :
The South—new-risen on the sea—
   A tremulous horizon-glow.

We mused, " Shall there be gallant guests
   Within our polar hermitage,
As on the shore where Franklin rests,
   And others, named in Glory's page ? "

And, " Shall the light we look on blaze
   Above such battles as have been,
In other countries   other days—
   The giants and the gods between ? "

Till one declared, " We live to-night
    In what shall be the poet's world:
The lands 'neath our Aurora's light
    Are as the rocks the Titans hurled.

" From southern waters, ice-enthralled,
    Year after year the rays that glance
Shall see the Desert shrink appalled
    Before the City's swift advance.

" Shall see the precipice a stair,
    The river as a road.   And then
There shall be voices to declare
    'This work was wrought by manly men.' "

And so our South all stately swept
    In vision past us, to and fro;
While stealthy winds of midnight crept
    About us, whispering fast and low.

Nearing Port.

A BLUE line to the westward that surely is not cloud;
A green tinge in the waters; a clamorous bird-crowd;
Then far-off foamy edges, and hill-tops timber fringed;
And, perched aloft, a light-house, o'er gray cliffs golden-
    tinged.

O watchers leaning landward, know ye of nothing more?—
And hear ye but the sea-birds?—and see ye but the shore?
Nay, look awhile, and listen who bids you welcome there;—
The great seas kiss her sandals, the high stars gem her hair!
Behold her in the gateway!—high-held in either hand
A blazing beacon—lighted to lead you to the land.

" Now welcome, kindly welcome, who come to me for cheer !
My forts may frown on others, but ye have nought to fear.
The cannon's flash and thunder are all for joy to-day —
No murmurs meet your coming —none wish to bar your way."

O, later called to labour, shall we who toiled at morn
Remember, as against you, the heat and burthen borne ?
No, verily, we shall not ! —We pray the labourer's Lord
May give you after-comers a full day's full reward.

Now fear not, fair-haired maiden, for gladness waits thee here,
As by thy father's fireside in bygone days and dear.

Thy troubled brow, O matron, beneath its silvering hair,
Shall gain no fresher furrows, shall lose its look of care ;
No longer for thy household the winter need'st thou dread,
Nor, fearing for to-morrow, shalt stint the children's bread.

And thou, a "mother's darling," on those young locks of
     thine
What midnight rains shall batter—what tropic suns shall
     shine !
Thy tender hands, toil-hardened, unwonted tools shall wield—
Shall fell the columned forest —shall till the furrowed field.
Yet, when at England's fireside her olden tales are told,
Perchance, 'mid tearful silence, one from the land of gold
Shall tell a brave new story —of want, and work, and care —
Of trial and of triumph — to touch the coldest there !

Now enter ye a haven your fathers have not known :
Now dwell ye in a country that once was not your own.
Part of the New World's army —the pioneers —are ye :
For whom there waits, ungathered, the wealth of earth and sea !
No need of " fiery baptism" — no blood, no tears to flow
Ah, legions of the Cæsars, had *you* but conquered so !
Ah, Vikings in Valhalla — our fathers dead and gone
Could *you* have made such landing such golden shores upon !

The Future of Australia.

SING us the Land of the Southern Sea—
   The land we have called our own;
Tell us what harvest there shall be
   From the seed that we have sown.

We love the legends of olden days,
   The songs of the wind and wave;
And border ballads and minstrel lays,
   And the poems Shakspeare gave—

The fireside carols and battle rhymes,
   And romaunt of the knightly ring;
And the chant with hint of cathedral chimes
   Of him "made blind to sing."

The tears they tell of our brethren wept,
   Their praise is our fathers' fame;
They sing of the seas our navies swept,
   Of the shrines that lent us flame.

But the Past is past—with all its pride—
   And its ways are not our ways,
We watch the flow of a fresher tide
   And the dawn of newer days.

Sing us the Isle of the Southern Sea—
   The land we have called our own;
Tell us what harvest there shall be
   From the seed that we have sown.

I see the Child we are tending now
    To a queenly stature grown ;
The jewels of empire on her brow,
    And the purple round her thrown.

She feeds her household plenteously
    From the granaries we have filled ;
Her vintage is gathered in with glee
    From the fields our toil has tilled.

The Old World's outcast starvelings feast,
    Ungrudged, on her corn and wine ;
The gleaners are welcome, from west and east,
    Where her autumn sickles shine.

She clothes her people in silk and wool
    Whose warp and whose woof we spun ;
And sons and daughters are hers to rule :
    And of slaves she has not one !

There are herds of hers on a thousand hills !
    There are fleecy flocks untold !
No foreign conquest her coffer fills—
    She has streams whose sands are gold !

She shall not scramble for falling crowns,
    No theft her soul shall soil ;
So rich in rivers, so dowered with downs,
    She shall have no need of spoil !

But if wronged or menaced she shall stand
    Where the battle surges swell,
Be a sword from Heaven in her swarthy hand
    Like the sword of La Pucelle !

If there be ever so base a foe
　　As to speak of a time-cleansed stain—
To say, " She was cradled long ago,
　　'Mid clank of the convict's chain ;"

Ask　as the taunt in his teeth is hurled—
　　" What lineage sprang she from
Who was Empress, once, of the Pagan World
　　And the Queen of Christendom !"

When the toilsome years of her youth are o'er,
　　And her children round her throng ;
They shall learn from her of the sage's lore,
　　And her lips shall teach them song.

Then of those in the dust who dwell
　　May there kindly mention be,
When the birds that build in the branches tell
　　Of the planting of the tree.

Wentworth.

'Tis a new thing for Australia that the waters to her bear
One who seeks not strength of sunshine, or the breath of
　　healing air :
One who recks not of her riches, nor remembers she is fair ;
One who land and houses, henceforth, holdeth not—for
　　evermore ;
Coming for such narrow dwelling as the dead need—to the
　　shore
Named aforetime by the spirit to receive the garb it wore.

'Tis a strange thing for Australia that her name should be
　　the name
Breathed ere death by one who loved her—claiming, with a
　　patriot's claim,
Earth of her as chosen grave-place; rather than the lands
　　of fame;
Rather than the Sacred City where a sepulchre was sought
For the noblest hearts of Europe; rather than the Country
　　fraught
With the incense of the altars whence our household gods
　　were brought.

'Tis a proud thing for Australia, while the funeral prayers
　　are said,
To remember loving service, frankly rendered by the dead;
How he strove, amid the nations, evermore to raise her
　　head;
How in youth he sang her glory, as it is, and is to be—
Called her " Empress "—while they held her yet as base-
　　born, over sea—
Owned her " Mother "　when her children scarce were
　　counted with the free !

How he claimed of King and Commons that his birthland
　　should be used
As a daughter, not an alien; till the boon, so oft refused,
Was withheld, at last, no longer; and the former bonds were
　　loosed.
How the scars of serfdom faded. How he led within the
　　light
Of her fireside Earth's Immortals; chrism-touched from
　　Olympus' height;
Whom gods loved; for whom the New Faith, too, has
　　guest-rooms garnished bright.

'Tis a great thing for Australia that her child of early years
Shared her path of desert-travel—bread of sorrow, drink
    of tears
Holding by her to these hill-tops, whence her Promised
    Place appears.
Titles were not hers to offer as the meed of service done;
Rank of peer or badge of knighthood, star or ribbon—she
    had none;
But she breathes a mother's blessing o'er the ashes of her
    son.

6th May, 1873.

The Fate of Bass.

A FANCY.

A.D. 180—

On the snow-line of the summit stood the Spaniard's English
    slave:
  And the frighted condor westward flew afar—
Where the torch of Cotopaxi lit the wide Pacific wave,
  And the tender moon embraced a new-born star.

Blanched the cheek that Austral breezes off Van Diemen's
    coast had tanned.
  Bent the form that on the deck stood stalwart there:
Slim and pallid as a woman's was the sailor's sunburnt
    hand,
  And untimely silver streaked the strong man's hair.

From the forest far beneath him came the baffled blood-
    hound's bay—
  From the gusty slope the camp-fire's fitful glow;
But the pass the Indian told of o'er the cliff beside him
    lay,
  And beyond—the Mighty River's eastward flow.

" Mine the secret of the Incas—to the tyrants never told :
  Mine the Cloven Rock—the league long Sculptured
    Way!
Ere the weary scouts awaken, ere the embers are grown
    cold—
  Ere the dogs in dreams their quarry seize and slay ! "

Freedom's threshold! —Yet he tarries—gazes seaward, south-
    ward still,
  Past the gulfs where fainting chain gangs toil entombed,
And the furnace of the smelter taints the winds of every hill
  With the fumes that swathe the dying and the doomed.

Never, never, gallant seaman, may the land that lit thy
    dreams,
  In the starless drive, make glad thine eyes again—
Where through tropic heavens at midnight the Antarctic
    glory streams,
  And a sea of blossom floods the wintry plain.

Nevermore the settler's welcome, at the sinking of the sun,
  Nor his godspeed 'mid the fragrant Austral morn !
Shattered, spent, and broken hearted— yet a guerdon thou
    hast won,
  And where brave souls meet thou shalt not stand forlorn.

Queensland to New South Wales.

26th JANUARY, 1888.

A CENTENNIAL GREETING.

Joy be with thee, Elder Sister, on thy proud Centennial
  Day —
All thy stalwart sons about thee, and thy daughters, dear as
  they,
And the sheaves of thy Thanksgiving gladdening with their
  golden glow
Lands that lay a globe unbroken but a hundred years ago!

Thou hast crowned thyself with cities — and no stone is built
  on Wrong :
Freemen tend thy flocks at pasture, freemen dwell thy hills
  among.
Never Ural, never Andes, held such wealth as is thine own —
By no sweat of serfdom tainted, purchased by no bondman's
  groan.

Nor for gain alone thy striving, nor to sit in place of pride :
Whilst thy roof-tree still was lowly, thou didst lodge in
  chambers wide
Learning, Charity, Religion — of thy hard-won store
  bestowed.
In each steep by thee surmounted thou hast hewn for them
  a road.

On the heights of wave-washed Sydney stand her stately
  College towers :
Far and wide full many a Hospice waits to soothe
  Misfortune's hours ;
From the Altar-fires thou kindledst there be brands already
  borne
To illume the Earth's dark places and to comfort the forlorn.

Joy be with thee, O our Sister!   We thy kin are glad with
    thee
For the greatness of thy Present— for the glory that shall be
When the Noblest of the Nations— SHE we all alike hold
    dear—
Calls thee not alone her DAUGHTER, but for evermore
    her PEER.

Melbourne International Exhibition.

A.D. 1880.

ARGUMENT.

I.—The House being ready, Victoria prepares to receive the nations whom she
has invited. They approach—the various countries of Europe, Asia, Africa, of the
American continent, the Australian colonies, and those of Polynesia—some of them
greater than any which ever paid tribute to Rome, or did homage to a mediæval
monarch, and their products superior to those which in olden times were fit gifts
from one king to another.

II.—Victoria salutes the other Australian colonies, and asks them to unite
with her in greeting her other guests. They then welcome the various countries
of Asia, Africa (Egypt to Caffraria, &c.), America (the South American Republics,
Empire of Brazil, Dominion of Canada, and the United States of North America);
then France, Spain, and Portugal; Italy, Greece, Russia, Switzerland; then
Holland and Belgium, Denmark, Austria, Germany, Norway and Sweden; then
Britain.

III.—The triumphs of Peace and of Toil.

IV.—Aspirations for the future of Australia that she may be happy, a
generous friend, but, if need be, a formidable enemy.

I.

CEASED is the sound of the chisel, and hushed is the
    hammer's ring,
And the echoes that haunted the empty halls for a while
    have taken wing:
And the doors are open, and overhead are a thousand flags
    unfurled,
While with music and song to the House she has built
    Victoria welcomes the world.

For the nations she bade with friendly voice have hearkened
    to her behest,
And treasure-laden, o'er land and sea, comes many an
    honoured guest—
Daughters of cultured Europe, deigning her day to grace—
Children of antique Asia—Africa's dusky race—
America's mighty offspring—and they of Australia's line—
And they of the Thousands Islands set where Pacific waters
    shine.
Oh, never a Roman triumph, nor court of mightiest
    Suzerain
Hath gathered such as have sailed to her. Nor gifts like to
    theirs have lain
At the feet of Wisdom's favoured one—when the Princes
    came from far,
And the swarthy Queen to the Great Sea steered by the
    light of the still pole star.

II.

Welcome, O fair five Sisters, unto your Sister's side!
Greet we this day together them who come from far and
    wide.

Come ye, aflame with jewels, and each with veiled face,
Whence bright eyes beam upon us like stars from cloud-
    swept space,
We wonder o'er the labours your slender hands have done
In ancient Asian cities, brown daughters of the sun!

And thou who once wast Pharoah's, and thou whose palm-
    thatched kraals
For centuries made marvel of bold De Gama's sails,
And all that dwell betwixt you, whate'er your race and
    name,
Who seek our shores in kindness, we thank you that you
    came.

And them who claim the treasures erewhile Pizarro's prize,
And her who crowned Braganza, the worthy and the wise,
And Canada we welcome, the loyal and the free,
And thee, O great Republic, with rule from sea to sea,
Who bravedst for our lost ones the fatal frozen main,
Thou who has fed our famished and wept above our slain.

Fair France, we greet thee fondly as our Crusader sires
Thy knightly sons saluted by Acre's stubborn spires!
O brave in war! none brighter in peaceful arts doth shine!
Arachne's fairy fingers are not more deft than thine!

And ye, the Goth's twin daughters, of stately mien and
        speech,
Spain and her queenly neighbour, a loving hand to each!
Long may thy sons be worthy the Cid's illustrious name;
And thine another Lusiad writ on the rolls of fame!

Italia! as we greet thee, our hearts are all aglow,
What centuries of glory thou knowest and shalt know!
Thine are the Roman eagles, the lilies Florentine,
The sea wed city's lion, the Church's Conquering Sign!

And Greece, we do thee reverence, who on Olympian seat
Art goddess yet; earth's greatest but learners at thy feet!

Now gladly we receive thee, within unguarded gate,
O upward-toiling Russia —whose lamp, though lit but late,
Already cheered thy children. What berg-blocked sea is
        thine!
God grant thee open water beyond its Arctic line!

And welcome here, Helvetia —from heights where peace abides
Beyond the wreck-strewn floodmark of battle's crimson tides:

Thou pliest, busy-fingered, each harmless handicraft,
Yet, ready in thy quiver there rests the patriot shaft.

And ye whom frugal Flanders has dowered with all her
     store —
Her old cathedral cities, her freedom won of yore —
When by the hands that raised them, her dykes asunder
     torn,
Swift poured the burgher's vengeance for Egmont and for
     Horn.
And thou whose peerless Princess, pure as thy Baltic foam,
Is dear in ancient Windsor as in her Danish home —
(For where thy raven reached not, thy dove hath found
     her rest,
And in the heart of England hath made herself a nest!)
Thou, dweller by the Danube—thou, keeper of the Rhine;
Thou, blue-eyed Scandinavia, with fragrant crown of pine;
All — all who followed Odin, the leader and the priest,
From bondage and from darkness in some forgotten East,
And tilled the trackless forest, and tamed the wild North sea,
Account us as your kindred — for kin, in truth, are we!

And now to her we hasten, with daughterly embrace,
To whom young isles do homage, and empires old give place,
And every zone pays tribute of wealth, and earth, and wave,
The refuge of the alien, the champion of the slave!
On triple throne unshaken as adamantine wall,
Long may'st thou sit, Britannia, dear mother of us all!

III.

Mighty ones, who have hither borne your trophies manifold,
We honour them who have earned you these, as we honour
     your great of old,

Every worker with brain or hand—the artist—the artizan,
Whether he ride at an army's head, or march in the name-
    less van.
For bright is the ruddy shield of Mars, and sweet is the
    Sun-god's lyre;
But Labour beareth the world aloft on shoulders that will
    not tire.

IV.

Thou who givest the eye to see, and the ready hand to do,
And a nation's place in the earth's fair space, give us Thy
    blessing, too!
We hear the cool Antarctic winds in the golden wheatfields
    pipe,
And the chant the swart Kanaka sings where the rustling
    cane grows ripe -
And we ask of Thee, who hast dowered our land with the
    kindly sun and soil
Which fill with fruitage of farthest climes the hopeful hands
    of toil.
That ever in love we may nurture, too, the people which
    dwelt apart,
When they seek new life from our Younger World and a
    home within her heart.
And if, perchance, from the caves of peace and the sheltering
    olive bough,
Our sons shall sail to a stormy sea and the shock of the mail-
    clad prow,
May they show that not in vain they have borne the stress
    of the tropic day,
Or lain, toil-spent, in the miner's tent, or made in the wilds
    a way.

"Australasian," 2nd October, 1880.

II.

Victoria.

1837—1887.

The Heralds gave to English air a new un-English name :
The Standard soared above the roof, the swart guns flowered
     in flame :
And London—East and West—awatch, saluted as she
     came
Girl-Queen of immemorial race—the Heir of Alfred's fame.

" And will she love like Eleanor who shared great Edward's
     throne ?
Or reign, like proud Elizabeth—her Country's Bride alone ?
Shall ever blot through her befall ? or shade of shame be
     blown
On England's name—to Englishmen yet dearer than their
     own ? "

   *   *   *   *   *   *   *

Fair Record of the Fifty Years that she has worn the
     Crown—
What royal name in scrawl antique on charter frayed and
     brown
Bears homelier sound to-day than hers ?—is richer in
     renown ?
What honour needs Victoria now from her dead kin brought
     down ?

𝖂ilhelm II.

1888.

Thy grandsire's sword is thine to-day,
  Thy noble father's crown unworn;
The realm where strong Charlemagne held sway,
  The name by Barbarossa borne.

Where toiled these mighty harvesters,
  What martial fame remains to win?
Gleaning, perchance, of knightly spurs,
  O Heir of many a Paladin!

Yet, need the hope be wholly vain
  That Heaven no less for thee prepares
The call to arms, the grand campaign,
  The laurel—evergreen as theirs?

Yon sullen ember—Discontent—
  Gleams deadlier than the Gallic brand!
(The Hopeless on the pillars leant,
  And Ruin kissed his beckoning hand.)

The Empire woven of old was knit
  With hostile tribe and hated clan;
And feudal foes the camp-fires lit,
  And marched as comrades to Sedan.

So, Kaiser, to *thy* Councils call
  The Chiefs. Bid Freedom's friends be thine—
Thy trusted allies, welcome all—
  From Thames or Tiber, Seine or Rhine!

Then they and thou the war may wage,
  O Son of Heroes, unafraid—
Though hosts invisible engage,
  And they be Legion which invade.

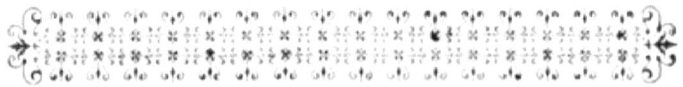

III.

Charles Dickens.

1870.

ABOVE our dear Romancer's dust
  Grief takes the place of praise,
Because of sudden cyprus thrust
  Amid the old-earned bays.

Ah! when shall such another friend
  By England's fireside sit,
To tell her of her faults, yet blend
  Sage words with kindly wit?

He brings no pageants of the past
  To wile our hearts away;
But wins our love for those who cast
  Their lot with ours to-day.

He gives us laughter glad and long;
  He gives us tears as pure;
He shames us with the published wrong
  We meted to the poor.

Through webs and dust and weather-stains,
  His sun like genius paints,
On life's transfigured chancel-panes,
  The angels and the saints.

He bade us to a lordly feast,
    And gave us of his best ;
And vanished, while the mirth increased,
    To be Another's guest.

For Death had summoned him, in haste,
    Where hands of the Divine
Pour out, for him who toiled to taste,
    The Paradisal wine.

Well, God be thanked, we did not wait
    His greatness to discern
By funeral lights—in that Too-Late
    When ashes fill the urn.

Gordon.

JANUARY, 1885.

DEVOTION !   When thy name is named,
    What matchless visions rise !
The Hebrew, leaving Pharoah's house,
    To Israel's rescue flies ;
The Moabitess gleans, content,
    Beneath the burning skies.

The flower of Christendom is given
    To gain the Holy Grave ;
O'er Acre and o'er Askelon
    The blessed banners wave ;
By Edward's bed I see thee kneel,
    O Queen beloved and brave !

Who art thou, girl, in warrior garb—
  St. Catherine's sword in hand?
'Tis La Pucelle—and France is free;
  O shame that thou must stand
Bound—helpless—at the cruel stake,
  To wait the headman's brand!

And now upon the wild North Sea
  From Lindisfarne's bleak shore,
To save the lives of shipwrecked men
  A maiden plies the oar;
Seamen and landsmen honour thee,
  Grace Darling, evermore!

And swifter, closer, as I muse,
  The splendid spectres loom;
And stately stands among them one
  To glory passed from gloom—
But late—by waters of the Nile—
  In walls of lost Khartoum!

Tolstoi.

A SHABBY volume on the ledge;
  An idle hand that drew it forth;
Like him who slumbered in the sedge,
  There dwelt the Prophet of the North.

Wayfarer!—Erst with hasty tread
  The paths of Story wont to trace—
What glamour on thine eyes is shed
  That fain thou lingerest in the place?

Methought the Masters all were gone,
    Or quenched their fires—by age besnowed;
Yet now, behold, a light hath shone;
    Once more a message is bestowed!

From shores held sterile there hath sailed
    A galleon filled with richest freight.
O truthful picture slow unveiled!
    O precious word long untranslate!

We gazed—yet scarce might understand.
    We hearkened—to the voice alone.
We praised the labour of his hand,
    And still his heart remained unknown.

We drank with him the joy of Spring;
    In Cossack foray learnt to ride;
With him we heard the gipsies sing—
    The cannon by the Euxine tide.

Then—sleepless in the hour when none
    Save humankind unslumbering lie—
When stars are pallid and the sun
    Unlit, and weaklings faint and die—

With sudden skill we read the rune—
    All tremulous and yet elate—
" Dread thou no dole; crave thou no boon;
    Be Duty unto thee as Fate!"

May, 1889.

IV.

Morituri te Salutant.

1870.

The *coup d'etat* is blotted out
  With fresher blood, with blacker crime—
As midnight horrors put to rout
  The vaguer ghosts of twilight-time.

" Greeting from those who are to die ! —
  Hail Cæsar ! " — *Draw the curtains round.*
In vain ! — That mournful mocking cry
  Pierces the purple with its sound.

And they who raise it enter too —
  With spectral looks and noiseless tread—
Unbidden, hold their dread review,
  Beside the Emperor's very bed.

They sought in his deserted tent ;
  They found him in the German camp.
They tarry till the oil be spent
  That feeds his life's poor flickering lamp.

The hope of France — the " gilded youth "—
  So answering the trumpet's peal
As if revealing how, in sooth,
  The gilding oft o'erlies the steel!

Soldiers Algeria's sun has spared :
  Heroes from Russia's fire and frost ;
Gray veterans—scarred and scanty-haired—
  Who wept at word of eagles lost.

Workmen, who leave the rattling looms
  To ply, perforce, a deadlier trade ;
Students, who quit their cloudy rooms
  To step within a heavier shade.

Slow-breaking hearts that suffer long—
  Blinded and chilled 'neath love's eclipse ;
Singing no more the happy song
  By horror frozen on their lips.

From castled cities battle-proof,
  They press to the accusing ranks
From cottage walls—from canvas roof—
  Ere passing to the Stygian banks.

The thousands famine yet shall waste
  The holocaust disease will claim—
As to God's Judgment-Bar they haste,
  They gaze on him who is to blame.

" Hail Cæsar ! "—While Napoleon's star
  From yon horizon beams " Farewell ! "
Setting in exile where, afar,
  The children of St. Louis dwell.

Come from the past—once dreaded ghosts,
  Whose number and whose names he knew !
The future plants at countless posts
  Sentries more terrible than you !

Napoleon III.

9TH JANUARY, 1873.

Its silent spirit from the place
    Slid forth unseen; amid the throng
Of those whose love outlived disgrace—
    Whose fealty to the last was strong.
'Midst homage, 'neath Fate's adverse reign,
    Paid to the star shorn of its rays
How passed the Exile? Lingering fain –
    As never once in prouder days?

The Mother and the Child were there
    Discrowned and disinherited!
No hand henceforth to right the heir;
    New griefs to bow the golden head.
How passed Napoleon? Prizing more
    Old fame in camp and council won,
Or fearless England's ægis o'er
    The future of her ally's son?

Gate of that World we know not yet—
    What thou beheld'st who may proclaim?
Were spirit-ranks in order set,
    Haunting thy portals as he came,
With voices murmuring: "Our life-torch—
    Unspent was quenched at his behest"?
Did bygone princes fill the porch—
    Bourbon, and Valois, and the rest?

How passed the soldier?—Cold and stern—
    'Mid weaponless reproachful ghosts—
As when he lead them forth to learn
    How fight the hardy German hosts?

How passed the Emperor where THEY gazed—
   Once wearers of the ancient crown?
As one who knew its lustre blazed
   The brighter ere he laid it down?

How passed he? — brighter grows the dream!
   Past yon accusing spirit-band —
Beyond the scornful Old Régime—
   Another group of watchers stand!
Those hands are stretched to greet him now
   That once Charlemagne's proud sceptre won;
While hastes Hortense with beaming brow—
   No longer banished from her son!

To the White Julienne.

" The white Julienne remains the flower of Marie Antoinette."—
                              ALPHONSE KARR.

AGAIN above thy fragile flowers
   I bend, to bring their perfume nigh;
For only in the evening hours
   Thy odours pass thy blossoms by;
But, when the ministering day
   Deserts thee with the warmth and light
That lulled thee, waking thou wilt pay
   For these, in sweetness, to the night.

O flower of Marie Antoinette!
   Ungrateful to the lavish day—
Refusing it thy fragrance—yet
   Relenting in such generous way—

Perchance, like thee, while life was bright
   Her soul no holy savour shed —
Yet scattered incense when grief's night
   Wept dews of blood upon her head!

I bend to bring thy perfume near
   Again—I cannot leave the spot;
Damp walls and prison gloom are here!
   The beauties of the garden-plot
Are gone – save thee, White Julienne,
   Fond-handled by the fated queen!
I hear her sigh above thee—then
   The sentry's tread behind the screen!

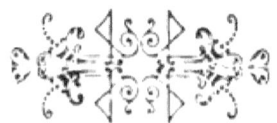

V.

To Henry the Fifth,

NAMED KING OF FRANCE, A.D. 1873.

Translated from the French of Victor Hugo.

My youth was passing, Sire, whilst you among
The cradle-wrappings slept : my morning-song
Sung o'er your pillow.   Winds of heaven have thrown
Us both, since then, on heights apart and lone.
Heights !   For misfortune drear, our destined land,
So thunder-scarred, a-nigh to heaven must stand !
The north and south are nearer than our ways
Are near to one another ; and Fate lays
The purple round you, and has not withheld
Our France's sceptre—dazzlements of eld.
I, crowned with silver hairs, say—praising you—
"Well done !"   That man is to his manhood true
Who bravely, at his own behest, will do
High deeds of self-undoing ; will forego
All—all—save immemorial honour ; - though
She seem to earthlier eyes a phantom, more
Will follow her (as erst in Elsinore
One faithful heart obeyed the beckoning ghost),
Nor stoop to buy a kingdom at her cost.
That you are aught save honest, none may say ;
The Lily must be white—all white—for aye.
A Bourbon can but reign as Capet's heir,
Or waive his kingship.   History is aware
Of wrecks enough - of changing battles' din—
Of those who grandly lose, or basely win !
Better with honour, Prince, the throne to quit
Than, where St. Louis sat, dishonoured sit !

The Pilgrimage to Kevlaar.

From the German of Heinrich Heine.

I.

THE mother stood at her window ;
    The sun on his pillow lay :
"Arouse thee, arouse thee, Wilhelm,
    For the pilgrims pass this way !"

" I hear not the holy songs, mother ;
    I see not the banners wave ;
My heart is like lead within me,
    For Gretchen is in her grave."

" No more of the Paternoster ;
    No more of the rosary :
We will go to God's Mother at Kevlaar,
    And thy heart-hurt healed shall be !"

The sacred banners are waving
    And the hymn rings clear and high
In Cologne Cologne of the Rhineland –
    As the pilgrim-host goes by.

And the mother and son together
    In the ranks are marching now ;
And their voices are swelling the chorus :
    " Hail Mary ! Praised be thou !"

II.

The Mother of God at Kevlaar
   In her richest robes is drest ;
From the multitude's prayerful clamour
   All day she will have no rest.

All day, as the sick salute her,
   Their gold and their silver ring ;
And feet and hands of the snow-white wax
   To her blessèd shrine they bring.

And whoso upon her altar
   A waxen limb doth lay,
From his limb of flesh doth Our Lady take
   The pain and the ail away.

   *   *   *   *   *   *

The mother she mouldeth a taper—
   She mouldeth it to a heart :
" Now bear it unto God's Mother,
   And Sorrow and thou shalt part ! "

The son with a sigh receives it ;
   With a sigh to Our Lady goes ;
The tears all-sorrowful streaming
   As the prayer all-sorrowful flows.

"O merciful One and mighty,
   And Maiden of God for aye!
O Mary, Queen of Heaven,
   Before thee my grief I lay!

"We dwell in Cologne of the Rhineland,
   My good old mother and I
Cologne of the thousand churches;
   And Gretchen lived close by;

"And now she is dead, O Mary!
   And I bring this heart—and I vow
If mine thou wilt heal I will ever say:
   'Hail, Mary! Praisèd be thou!'"

III.

The pilgrim-son and the mother
   In their narrow lodging slept;
And the Mother of God she entered—
   With a noiseless foot she stept;

And she bent o'er the broken-hearted
   With a pitiful pitiful smile—
Laying her hand so tender
   Over his heart the while.

Even so was vouchsafed the Vision
   To the mother—ere she sprang
From her couch at the watch-dog's 'larum
   Which loud and untimely rang.

And there, in the little chamber,
   Behold, her son lay dead!
His face—so pallid aforetime—
   A-flush with the morning-red.

Then his cold cold hands the mother
   Folded—she knew not how—
And, as erst, devout she murmured:
   "Hail Mary! Praised be thou!"

December, 1885.

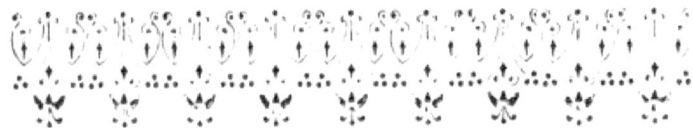

VI.

The Belated Swallow.

" And the birds of the air have nests."

BELATED swallow, whither flying?
The day is dead, the light is dying,
  The night draws near:
Where is thy nest, slow put together,
Soft-lined with moss and downy feather,
For shelter place in stress of weather
  And darkness drear?

Past, past, above the lighted city,
Unknowing of my wondering pity,
  Seaward she flies.
Alas, poor bird! what rude awaking
Has driven thee forth, when storms are breaking,
And frightened gulls the waves forsaking
  With warning cries?

Alas, my soul! while leaves are greenest
Thy heedless head thou fondly screenest
  Beneath thy wing.
How bravely thou thy plumage wearest
How lightly thou life's burthen bearest
How happily thy home preparest
  In careless spring!

Yet days to come an hour may bring thee
When none of all that sing can sing thee
   To joy or rest !
When all the winds that blow shall blow thee ;
And, ere the floods shall overflow thee,
The sunlight linger but to show thee
   Thy shattered nest !

𝔚𝔞𝔰𝔥𝔢𝔡 𝔄𝔰𝔥𝔬𝔯𝔢.

HAVE you heard of the fate of the albatross?
   Of the bird that was washed ashore ?
And the message to tell of a good ship's loss
   That around his neck he bore !

I have heard of the bird that was washed ashore—
   Of the crew that were cast away ;
And the Crozet rocks and the ocean roar
   Have haunted me all the day.

Yet not of the wreck have I mused forlorn,
   Nor the Isle in the Indian sea :
And not for the drifting dead I mourn,
   " In the haven where they would be."

   *   *   *   *   *   *

A speck that seems as it scarce had stirred
   A blur on the blue wave's crest—
The wide wide wings of a gallant bird—
   The gleam of his white white breast.

He was fledged where the sunless oceans flush
　　To the sudden crater glow,
And at dead of night the Aurora's blush
　　Comes back from the Polar snow.

No smoke of the city had smirched his wings;
　　No young of the flock he stole;
No nest of his to the rafters clings;
　　Of the fields he took no toll.

*　　*　　*　　*　　*　　*

O Spirit heedless of wealth and state—
　　One hour was thy star ashine,
When by Nature's side thou didst walk elate,
　　With thy First Love's hand in thine!

*　　*　　*　　*　　*　　*

How was it, O bird, when thy bosom warm
　　'Neath an icy grip grew chill?
And the wings were furled that defied the storm,
　　And the fluttering heart grew still?

Could the far Antarctic lights illume
　　The blackness of sky and sea
When Fate held thee helpless amid the gloom
　　That rose 'twixt thy Past and thee?

1st October, 1887.

In the South Pacific.

A VISION of a savage land,
　A glimpse of cloud-ringed seas :
A moonlit deck, a murderous hand ;—
　No more, no more of these !

No more ! how heals the tender flesh,
　Once torn by savage beast ?
The wound, re-opening, bleeds afresh,
　Each season at the least !

O day, for dawn of thee-how prayed
　The spirit, sore distressed !
Thy latest beams, upslanting. made
　A pathway for the blest.

And robes, new-donned, of the redeemed,
　Gleamed white past grief's dark pall :
So this, a day of death which seemed,
　A birthday let us call.

Remembering, such day as this,
　A soul from flesh was shriven,
By death, God's messenger of bliss :
　A spirit entered Heaven.

Thy dying head no loving breast
　Upheld, O early slain ;
But soon, 'mid welcoming saints, 'twas prest
　Where God's own Child has lain !

Though none at death broke Bread for thee,
    Or poured the Sacred Wine;
Thou, nourished at His Board, dost see
    The Substance of the Sign.

We mourned *thee!* Heaven's new born, and rich
    Past all our prayers could claim,
Secure in blessedness, of which
    We have not learnt the name.

No Message.

SHE heard the story of the end,
    Each message, too, she heard;
And there was one for every friend;
    For her alone—no word.

And shall she bear a heavier heart,
    And deem his love was fled;
Because his soul from earth could part
    Leaving her name unsaid?

No—No!—Though neither sign nor sound
    A parting thought expressed—
Not heedless passed the Homeward-Bound
    Of her he loved the best.

Of voyage-perils, bravely borne,
　　He would not tell the tale ;
Of shattered planks and canvas torn,
　　And war with wind and gale.

He waited till the light-house star
　　Should rise against the sky ;
And from the mainland, looming far,
　　The forest scents blow by.

He hoped to tell — assurance sweet !—
　　That pain and grief were o'er —
What blessings haste the soul to meet,
　　Ere yet within the door.

Then one farewell he thought to speak
　　When all the rest were past —
As in the parting hour we seek
　　The dearest hand the last.

And while for this delaying but
　　To see Heaven's opening Gate —
Lo, it received him — and was shut
　　Ere he could say " I wait."

Sonnets.

I.

CHRISTMAS DAY.

O HAPPY day, with seven-fold blessings set
Amid thy hallowed hours—the memories dear
Of childhood's holidays—and household cheer,
When friends and kin in loving circle met
And youth's glad gatherings, where the sands were wet
By waves that hurt not, whilst the great cliffs near,
With storms erewhile acquaint, gave echo clear
Of voices gay and laughter gayer yet.
And graver thoughts and holier arise
Of how, 'twixt that first eve and dawn of thine,
The Star ascended which hath lit our skies
More than the sun himself; and 'mid the kine
The Child was born whom shepherds, and the wise
Who came from far, and angels, called Divine.

II.

THE NEW YEAR.

WITH supple boughs and new-born leaflets crowned,
Rejoicing in fresh verdure stands the tree,
Though weather-scarred and scooped by fire may be
Its ancient trunk.   So may our lives be found
(God leaving still our roots within His ground),
Where gaps of loss and waste show brokenly
May each new year that comes to greet us see
Branches, and foliage, and flowers abound.
Where Fortune, spoiling wayfarer, hath left
Unsightly rents, may garlands spring apace.
And if, perchance, some pitiless wind hath reft
Away what newer green shall ne'er replace,
May heaven-light come the closer for the cleft
O'er which no tender fronds shall interlace.

Watch-Night.

MIDNIGHT   musical and splendid —
And the Old Year's life is ended;
And the New, "born in the purple," babe yet crowned,
among us dwells;
While Creation's welcome swells—
Starlight all the heavens pervading,
And the whole world serenading
Him, at birth, with all its bells!

Round the cradle of the tender
Flows the music, shines the splendour;
It is early yet for counsel,—but bethink how Hermes gave —
(While the Myths were bright and brave)—
Thwarted Phœbus no small battle,
Seeking back his lifted cattle —
Hour-old Hermes, in his cave!

New Year, if thy youth should blind us
Thy swift feet, perchance, may find us
Sleeping in the dark — unguarded as the sun-god's herds
were found!
Lest, unready, on his round
We be hurried —World, take warning
That already it is morning
And a giant is unbound!

Idle-handed yet, but willing,
Let us ponder ere the filling
Of his empty eager fingers with our heedless hot behest.
Be our failures frank-confessed
'Mid the gush of gladsome greeting
Requiem in our hearts repeating
For the years that died unblest.

How they came to us – so precious ! --
How abode with us so gracious !—
Blindly doing all our bidding ; stronger, swifter, than we
thought.
Like the sprites by magic brought ;
Shaping dream to action for us ;
Till we stood, beset with sorrows,
Wondering what ourselves had wrought !

Ere the tightening of the tether
Bind this year and us together,
Let us pause awhile and ponder : Whither tend we side by
side —
He who gallops – we who guide ?—
Once we start like lost Lenore
Sung in Bürger's ballad-story -
Fast as Odin's hunt — we ride !

VII.

David's Lament for Jonathan.

Thou wast hard pressed, yet God concealed this thing
  From me; and thou wast wounded very sore,
And beaten down, O son of Israel's king,
  Like wheat on threshing-floor.

Thou, that from courtly and from wise for friend
  Didst choose me, and in spite of ban and sneer,
Rebuke and ridicule, until the end
  Didst ever hold me dear!

All night thy body on the mountain lay:
  At morn the heathen nailed thee to their wall.
Surely their deaf gods hear the songs to-day
  O'er the slain House of Saul!

Oh! if that witch were here thy father sought,
  Methinks I e'en could call thee from thy place,
To shift thy mangled image from my thought,
  Seeing thy soul's calm face.

I sorrowed for the words the prophet spoke,
  That set me rival to thy father's line;
But o'er thy spirit no repining broke
  For what had else been thine.

Thou wast not like to me, so rude, so hot ;
  The world was not in thine, as in my sight,
Like the proud giant who from Israel sought
  A champion to fight.

I thought to ask nor looked to be denied
  Of God, that in my days there might ascend
His House ; not from my hands, so redly dyed,
  But thine, pure-hearted friend.

My friend, within God's House thou dwellest now ;
  Thy wounds are healed thou need'st no Gilead-balm ;
Defeated and degraded, yet thy brow
  Is crowned with death and calm.

O God, this is Thy black and bitter sea
  Which buffets so and blinds my struggling soul :
Out of the depths I cry, O God, to Thee,
  Whose grief-waves o'er me roll.

God give to me the spirit that was his—
  The patience, that he needs no more to blend
With the wild eagerness that mars my bliss ;
  I would be like my friend.

Through the dark valley soon, to where he stands,
  God summon me ! Till then the sword shall shine
That comes from his dead grasp into my hands ;
  His children be as mine !

At the Fords of Jordan.

The parting of King David and Barzillai the Gileadite after the revolt of Absalom.

A LITTLE way farther to guide thee I go
Where the footing is firm and the waters are low ;
Then we part, O my King, thou once more to thy throne,
I to dwell, in the house of my fathers—alone.

Yet think not, O David, one pang of regret
Would tempt the recall of the youth I have set
In thy presence ; the strong-armed, the true-hearted one –
Last gift of my loyalty— even my son.

Ere my hand to the husbandman's toil had been trained,
Or my foot to the slow-moving flocks had been chained,
I, too, would have marched in the long line of spears—
With the youthful, the courtly, the brave for my peers.

The days when I dreamt but of battle !—The lamp
Which all night I kept burning—that, if from the camp
One straggler should come, I might hang up his sword
And hearken how prospered the cause of the Lord !

How my heart used to beat ; how my veins used to thrill
From freezing to fever, from fever to chill,
When the voice of the Philistine rang through our coasts,
Defying   unanswered – the Lord God of Hosts !

How I prayed day and night— ay, with many a tear –
" Lord, shorten the time till Thy champion appear ! "
And if fearing or hoping myself to change blows
With the giant—God bidden— I know ; and God knows !

Ah, it was not for gain, and it was not for fear,
That I wore not the warrior's glittering gear :—
My father, my mother ! the heart-strife was done !
For Saul had his thousands and they had but one.

I am old, but, King David, I cannot forget
My hot-hearted youth ; so my boy shall not fret
'Mid the safety and sameness of flocks and of fields
While the soldiers of Israel burnish their shields.

The Lord be thy keeper, henceforth and for aye,
My son whom I love !—And when I am away
Be thy spirit as now pure and lofty, and bold ;
Thy strength still unwasted ; thy heart never cold.

When thy soul with the minions of darkness must fight,
The Great King lend thee weapons and armour of light.
No hindrance are they like the harness of Saul
To the boy from the folds. May'st thou bear them through
          all !

All blessings be thine which the promise foretells !
And, oh, when the heart of thy eldest born swells
At thy stories of many a soldierly deed,
Tell how one, not a soldier, served Israel in need.

The men are fast forming again into rank ;
The river is forded ; we part on the bank.
Haste where welcome awaiteth thee, David, this day ;
For the joy of the people ill beareth delay !

The Lord give thy children the love-guarded crown,
When the King and his servant in dust have lain down !
Till the hope of the nations thy lineage shall close—
God's arrows be sharp in the hearts of thy foes !

The Magi to the Star.

I.
THANKSGIVING.

Star, on thy Heaven-returning way,
    Our message of thanksgiving bear
To Him who answered with thy ray
    The priestless Gentiles' trembling prayer.

When songs of revel shook the roof,
    God, Thou didst cheer the joyless course,
Where we, like Vashti, walked aloof,
    Braving the world's unjust divorce.

How rate we now all griefs and scorn
    That filled our youth with bitterness!
We had not known the Christ is born
    But that we sought for One to bless!

II.
PRAYER.

Fence Thou Thy Child, O Merciful,
    When hate shall cavil at His worth;
When underlings like Haman rule
    Hold Thou the golden sceptre forth.

When envy round Thy Precious One
    Its tongues of scorching flame hath curled,
Unwasted let His virtue run
    From the sore furnace of the world

To fill a new Colossus-mould,
    When tireless unbelief hath sent
Thy truest Image to the cold
    Pure mountain-tops of banishment,

Give then, O God, Thy light, to break
   Through all earth's valleys cramped and dim,
That after-times may see, and take
   Their heroes' measurement from Him!

III.

FAREWELL.

A new horizon's dim blue ring
   Around our watch-fire shall be cast —
New stars replace the vanishing —
   To-morrow's homeward travel past.

Word-bringer, now thine embassy
   Is closed, thou stayest not to fill
A lowlier office. Thou shalt be
   Soon 'mid the angels, shining still!

One priceless pearl of upper sea—
   One matchless gem of heaven's rich mine:
Within the place once held by thee
   God send no after-light to shine!

Yet, foremost of the host of gold,
   Long-followed, thou wast never sent —
A glimpse of what the Heavens enfold
   To darken earth with discontent!

Star of the Promised! Streaming on
   Through Time's long night —though thou
      must set
Thy light shall spread, when thou art gone,
   O'er sunless lands we see not yet!

To the Virgin Mary.

MOTHER of Him we call the Christ,
   No halo round thy brows we paint—
Incense and prayer we offer not,
   Nor mind to title thee as saint.

And yet, no woman's name—of all
   With honour from the ages sent—
Mary, is aureoled like thine,
   With love and grief and glory blent!

Oh wisely was it that He chose—
   Who the unwritten future reads—
To teach the after-world, through thee,
   What cherishers Messiah needs.

Thou heard'st the angel's prophecy—
   The tidings which the shepherds brought—
Anna and Simeon praising God—
   And saw'st that star the Wise Men sought!

Ah, who of us could bear—like thee—
   With meekness, God's triumphal light;
Then—still believing, with His Charge—
   At midnight take an exile's flight!

Throughout the Son's long helplessness
   His good was to thine own preferred;
May we so serve; and still, like thee,
   Stand back to let His voice be heard!

Dispenser once of earthly things,
   Thy Best-Belovèd thou didst see;
God's hands for others blessing-full—
   Could we be poor and glad like thee?

Soul-pierced with sword-like agony—
   Not felon's taunt nor soldier's jest,
Beside the God-forsaken Cross,
   Could drive thee from it like the rest.

Christ's banner thou alone didst hold
  In face of all His foes displayed ;
Valiant through all defeat — and but
  Heart-stricken that He was betrayed.

Ah, Mary ! Could we stand, like thee,
  Steadfast ; and watch the vowed depart ;
And grieve for their defection less
  Than for the Saviour's wounded heart ?

How must thy God — who favour set
  On David once and kingly Saul,
And yet foresaw their wanderings,
  And loved them through and after all—

How must He seal the prophecy,
  Declaring thee for ever blest,
Whose whole life showed thy worthiness
  Of that pure Child thine arms had pressed !

O single-hearted one to kiss
  The lifeless and dishonoured head
Fondly as when its baby brow
  By angel wings was canopied !

O self-forgetful, to rejoice
  For that Heaven's entrance had been found
By the Belovèd ; thou content
  Thenceforth alone to close life's round !

In the bright future — sure, though far —
  Again, as once, the wide air rings
With praise to Christ ! Thy vigil ends,
  Meek daughter of a hundred kings !

Virgin, may we partake thy joy,
  When Heaven and loyal earth shall lay
At the pierced feet of David's son
  A crown He will not put away !

VIII.

POEMS FOR CHILDREN.

The Australiad.

'Twas brave De Quiros bent the knee before the King of
 Spain,
And "Sire," he said, "I bring thy ships in safety home
 again
From seas unsailed of mariner in all the days of yore—
Where reefs and islets, insect built, arise from ocean's floor.
And, sire, the land we sought is found – its coasts lay full in
 view
When homeward bound, perforce, I sailed, at the bidding of
 my crew.
* *Terra Australis* called I it; and linked therewith the
 name
Of Him who guideth, as of old, in cloud and starry flame.
And grant me ships again," he said, "and southward let me
 go –
A new Peru may wait thee there—another Mexico."

A threadbare suitor, year by year—"There is a land," said
 he:
While King and Court grew weary of this old man of the
 sea:
For there were heretics to burn, and Holland to subdue,
And England to be humbled (which this day remains to do).
O land he named—but never saw—his memory revere!
The gallant disappointed heart—let him be honoured here!

  Terra Australis, del Esperito Sancto, one of the New Hebrides.

Meanwhile the hardy Dutchman came – as ancient charts
    attest–
Hartog, and Nuyts, and Carpenter, and Tasman, and the
    rest,
But found not forests rich in spice, nor market for their
    wares,
Nor servile tribes to toil o'ertasked 'mid pestilential airs
And deemed it scarce worth while to claim so poor a
    continent,
But with their slumberous tropic isles thenceforward were
    content.

And then came Dampier, who, erewhile, upon the Spanish
    Main
For silver-laden galleons lurked – and great was his disdain.
Good ships, beside, from France were sent – good ships and
    gallant crews –
With Marion and D'Entrecasteaux and the far-famed La
    Perouse.
And still, of all who sought or saw, the voyages were vain
Australia ne'er was farm for boers nor mission field for
    Spain,
Nor fleur-de-lys nor tricolour was ever planted here
And Britain's flag to hoist was not for hands of buccaneer.

But to our lovely eastern coast, led by auspicious stars,
Came Cook, in the Endeavour, with his little band of tars
Who straight on shores of Botany old England's ensign
    reared,
With mighty din of musketry and noise of them that
    cheered.
And none of all his noble fleets who sixty years was king
A prize so goodly ever brought as that small ship did
    bring !

And who was he—the FIRST to find Australia passing
    fair?—
One who aforetime well had served his country otherwhere:
Who to the Heights of Abraham up the swift St. Lawrence
    led,
When on the moonless battle-eve the midnight oarsmen
    sped.
No worthier captain British deck before or since hath
    trod
He "never feared the face of man," but feared alway his
    God.
His crew he cherished tenderly, and kept his honour bright,
For with the helpless blacks he dealt as if they had been
    white.
A boy, erewhile, of lowly birth, self-taught, a poor man's
    son,
But a hero and a gentleman, if ever there was one!
And when at last, by savage hands, on wild Owyhee slain,
He left a deathless memory—a name without a stain!

'Tis but a hundred years ago—as nearly as may be—
Since good King George's vessel first anchored in Botany.
A hundred years!—Yet, oh, how many changes there have
    been!
Unclasp thy volume, History, and say what thou hast seen.

Old England and her colonies stand face to face as foes,—
And now their orators inveigh, and now their armies close.
In vain, our mother land, for once thy sword is drawn
    in vain,
Allies and enemies alike, *thy children* are the slain.
Though, save as victor, never 'twas thy wont to quit the
    field,
Relenting filled thy valiant heart and thou wast fain to
    yield.

Ah, well for loss of those fair States might King and
    Commons mourn!
There lay, in sooth, a goodly bough from England's rose-
    tree torn!
But *now* how deep its roots have struck — how stately stands
    the stem —
How lovely on its branches leaf and flower and dewy gem!
New life from that sore severance to our sister-scion came,
God speed thee, young America, we glory in thy fame!

The storm that shook the Western World now eastward
    breaks anew—
And, oh, how black the tempest is which blotteth out the
    blue!
And over thee, ill-fortuned France, what floods resistless roll,
A tidal wave of blood no pitying planet may control!
Like Samson toiling blind and bound to furnish food for
    those
Who light withheld and liberty, and mocked at all his woes,
So have thy people held their peace—so laboured—so have
    borne
The burden serfdom ever bears, the sorrow and the scorn.
But as with groping giant-hands he seized the pillars twain
And made Philistia's land one house of mourning for the
    slain,
So rise they, frenzied, at the last, by centuries of wrong,
And wreak a vengeance dreadful as their sufferings have
    been long,
The vile Bastille is overthrown, the Monarchy lies low,
The fetters of the Feudal Age are broken at a blow!

Of Poland parted for a prey dire Nemesis shall tell
When o'er the dead in Cracow's vault shall ring Oppression's
    knell!

Now Erin from her Sister-Isle awhile was fain to part—
For Strongbow's arrow rankled long within her wounded
    heart ;
And long by desecrated fane and fireless hearth she wailed,
Where brutal Ireton's Herod-host their murderous pikes
    had trailed.
Here shine the names she holdeth dear ; and prize them
    well she may—
Past soldiers of a Frankish prince, or peers of Castlereagh ;
The gifted ones who pled for her 'gainst bigotry and pride,
The gallant ones who died for her when young Fitzgerald
    died !

Enough, enough,—forbear to trace the record of the age,—
Where elder nations are inscribed, through each distressful
    page :
But hearken how,—for once, at least—without an army's
    aid—
A people's lines—the lines of her who holds the South—
    were laid !

Five thousand leagues of ocean 'twixt the old home and the
    new,
And lodging strait and scanty fare the weary voyage
    through.
And toil and hardship safely past, and crossed the perilous
    main,
Never to tread on English ground 'mid English friends
    again !
Yet men were found to dare it all—men, ay, and women
    too—
(Not only those exiled perforce, who ofttimes rose anew,—
Out-cast upon new earth—with hope, and heart, and vigour
    given,
By fresh surroundings, and His grace who bids the lost to
    Heaven)—

The brave, the fair, the gently-born, and Labour's life-long
    thrall,
Within those circling seas of ours there was a place for all.

For patient hands the woods to fell, the new-formed fields
    to till,
The huts to build, the scanty flocks and herds to guard
    from ill.
For bolder spirits, to forsake the sea-board settlement,
And learn the secret of the land where never white man
    went,
Through mountain-pass, and forest dark, and wide unsheltered
    plain,
Through fiery heat of summer, and through frost, and flood,
    and rain,
Unheeding thirst or hunger, or the shower of savage spears;
What soldiers e'er were braver than Australian pioneers?
What though it was by axe, and plough, and miner's oft-
    edged tool,
And tending sheep and kine through weary years—of
    hardship full—
The only victories we boast were by our fathers won?
The men who won them had prevailed where feats of arms
    were done!
Three generations born of her our Country now can tell,
And son, and sire, and grandsire, all in turn have served her
    well;
Not only with the sinewy arm, the hardened hand of toil,
That wrest their wealth from rifted rock and forest-cumbered
    soil—
By love of order and of law; by proffered boon to all
Of learning—in the township school and in the college hall;
By liberal leisure, well-bestowed, for sports of land and
    wave;
And by the faith preserved to us God to the Elders gave!

And now Britannia's household send her greetings—from
    beside
The icy streams of Canada—and islands scattered wide
Betwixt the two Americas—from Africa's sea-marge,
And where the race of Aurungzebe held empire rich and
    large,
And where amid New Zealand fern the English skylarks
    build,
And rosy children's sun-burnt hands with English flowers
    are filled—
And from our own Australia too—and all unite to say:
" Bind us to thee with stronger bonds than those we own
    to-day,
Give to our sons a place with thine—for each to each is
    peer—
And let them share thy councils, and the dangers that
    endear ;
And what the Olden Realm has been the Newer Realm
    shall be,
With a place in every freeman's heart and a port in every
    sea !"

    Dundee, Queensland, 1884.

The Lifeboat of Dieppe.

" Peace hath her victories, no less than war."

A FOGGY day in the Dover Strait,
  Two ships on the misty main ;
A crash—then a pitiful, pitiful cry
  From the shattered sinking twain.

One boat alone—from the davits cut
  By a fair haired boy—swung free
Of the whirlpool that sucked the swimmers down,
  And awhile she stood to sea.

Then swift, ere the surge had ceased to swell
 O'er the good ships gulfed below,
She sped to the help of the perishing
 As fast as the boy could row.

*   *   *   *   *   *

Ebb tide at morn on the coast of France;
 Like a mill race the Channel ran;
And there gazed to seaward from gay Dieppe
 A grey-haired fisherman.

"A boat!" he shouted; "an English boat!
 Look, look! She is swept to sea—
Loaded down to the water's edge –
 Haste, haste to her help with me!"

They rallied round him, a gallant crew,
 And the ready lifeboat bore;
But the good old mayor stayed their march—
 "'Twere vain on yon sea-less shore.

"One way I wot of: The docks are full
 Though the harbour-rocks lie bare;
I will open the floodgates for her, men—
 Will you launch the lifeboat there?

"I give no order. You know the risk,
 But the boat *may* live." And then
He gazed on their faces and they on his
 While one might, perhaps, count ten.

Then, with never a word, they ran the boat
 To the great dock's tideless brim,
And they sprang to their places and grasped their
   oars,
 And the shore and the sky grew dim.

For the sweep of a torrent bore them now
   With a force that none might stay,
Away from the watchers that lined the pier—
   From the harbour-bounds away;

Out, out to the Channel. And there, afar,
   Were those they had vowed to save—
Oarless and spent, on the racing tide
   That sped to the western wave.

   *   *   *   *   *   *

Soon, soon—the ghost of an English cheer—
   Embrace as of brothers born!
'Twas told in Paris that selfsame night,
   In London at early morn.

1855.

The Old Pony's Christmas.

JUST look where they've put me! There's grass to the knee,
The juiciest of saltbush, the shadiest tree;
And they fenced off this pocket on purpose for me.

Last night Frank (my *old* master) rode down on Kildare;
When I looked in his face I knew mischief was there -
And a flour-bag he tied to *my tree*, I declare!

My little new master came early to-day;
He is Frank, rising four, and his hair is like hay;
And he *does* love to order (but *I* don't obey!)

He came in the buggy; my mistress as well
(A "light weight," *I love her.* Her name once was "Nell"
But now 'tis "Mamma,"— *why* I never could tell.)

My *old* Frank (now " Papa ") drove them down with the bays
And (this family of mine really have such *nice* ways!)
They brought me the loveliest bundle of maize.

" I grew it myself, old grey Dolo, for you,"
Said small Frank, " but Mamma often watered it too ;
And we wish ' Merry Christmas' and ' How do you do?'"

Then he peeped in my "stocking" and soon dragged to light
The *grandest* new bridle! (His face *was* a sight!)
"Oh, Dolo!" he cried, " Santa Claus came last night!"

The Clever Cat.

THERE *was* a cat called William—
　The poorest ever seen ;
He would not go a-mousing—
　He played the tambourine.

His family would not feed him—
　This lazy little cat—
But out of doors they turned him ;
　There seemed no way but that.

So on and on he wandered
　Till he to Catland came,
And there he met a Princess—
　Felina was her name.

She had the loveliest whiskers ;
　Her eyes were emerald green.
She fell in love with William—
　All for his tambourine !

For her delight was dancing
   And there was none to play.
"Strike up!" she straight commanded
   When William came that way.

All day she danced.   At sunset
   Poor William at her feet
Fell down and said, "Pray may I
   Have something now to eat?"

"To eat?   Of course!—What ho, there!"
   (Felina had no bell,
But when she called her servants
   Her sweet voice did as well.)

Then tortoiseshells and tabbies
   Tripped o'er each other's tails;
All scurrying from the kitchen
   With cream-cakes and stewed snails.

Now after this they brought him
   Six dinners every day—
And "mouse" was never mentioned.
   His brothers came to stay.

For *they* had heard of Catland
   Where William's word was law.
And by-and-by Felina
   Bestowed on him her paw.

There *is* a cat called William—
   The fattest ever seen;
He need not go a mousing –
   He plays the tambourine!